Little Grey's
Birthday Surprise

15.06.18.

Dear Baby Boy Shaw,

Happy Birthday to you!!
Welcome to this wonderful
world — we are so
happy that you are
here and so very
proud to be your
Uncle & Aunty!
We can't wait to
take you on
adventures,
jump in puddles
with you, buy
you ice creams,
read you stories,
and surround you with
love. always.
May your life be full of magic!
Uncle Neale & Aunty Holly x.x.

For Alex, Nora & Wilf, Noah & Hattie,
Zoë & Felix, James & Mollie –
Karl Newson

For Baby Kaszás and her mummy –
Louise Pigott

This edition published by Parragon Books Ltd in 2018

Parragon Books Ltd
Chartist House
15–17 Trim Street
Bath BA1 1HA, UK
www.parragon.com

Written by Karl Newson
Illustrated by Louise Pigott
Edited by Lily Holland
Designed by Kathryn Davies

ISBN 978-1-5270-1811-2

Printed in China

Little Grey's
Birthday Surprise

PaRragon

Bath • New York • Cologne • Melbourne • Delhi
Hong Kong • Shenzhen • Singapore

On the morning of Little Grey's birthday
he awoke with a "Hop hop hooray!"

He crunched his breakfast carrot
and he hopped outside to play.

He beamed the biggest smile
with his fluffy ears raised high.

"Come back home for lunch!" said Mum.
"We're having carrot pie!"

He bounded through the butterflies
and flowers in the sun.

Then all the way to Fox's house
to have some birthday fun.

DO NOT
DISTURB

'Do not disturb' read Fox's door,
perhaps he was asleep?

So Little Grey went on his way,
hop! skip! leap!

His fluffy ears weren't quite so high
as he bounced through rays of light.
Then all the way to Squirrel's house,
but…

…Squirrel was out of sight.
'Not at home' read Squirrel's door,
could she be at the shop?

Not at
home
x

So Little Grey went on his way,
boing! bounce! hop!

His fluffy ears fell lower
as he jumped through fields of green.
Then all the way to Bear's house,
but…

...Bear was nowhere to be seen.

'Out all day' the notice read,
but where could Bear have gone?

Little Grey's ears drooped
down,
down,
down…

...and he sighed.
"Where is everyone?"

He felt so sad all on his own,
so lonely and so small.
"My friends have forgotten my birthday.
This isn't fun at all!"

"hello!"

He called them in his
loudest voice...

...but there was no reply.

He curled himself up in a ball.
A tear fell from his eye.

Then he felt a tingle,
from his nose down to his tail.

Great big

footprints on the ground...

Bear had left a trail!

A trail that led through fields of green,

and back through rays of light,

back through flowers and butterflies,

to a happy, hoppy sight...

Surprise!

Squirrel, Bear and Fox had planned
a party all along!
All his friends were there with Mum
to sing his birthday song.

A bouncy castle, cake and hats,
the fun went on all day!

Little Grey beamed the
biggest smile and cheered,

"Hop hop hooray!"